Happy Ever After

ORCHARD BOOKS
338 Euston Road, London NW1 3BH
Orchard Books Australia
Level 17/207 Kent Street, Sydney, NSW 2000

First published in hardback in 2010 by Orchard Books
First published in paperback in 2011

ISBN 978 1 40830 753 3 (HB)
ISBN 978 1 40830 759 5 (PB)

Text © Tony Bradman 2010
Illustrations © Sarah Warburton 2010

A CIP catalogue record for this book is available from the British Library.

1 3 5 7 9 10 8 6 4 2 (HB)
1 3 5 7 9 10 8 6 4 2 (PB)

Printed in Great Britain

Orchard Books is a division of Hachette Children's Books,
an Hachette UK company.
www.hachette.co.uk

Tony Bradman

Happy Ever After

SNOW WHITE
AND THE MAGIC MIRROR

Illustrated by Sarah Warburton

ORCHARD BOOKS

Snow White was standing in front of an empty canvas with a brush in her hand.

She had been looking forward to this
so much! Painting pictures was her
passion, although somehow it seemed
she could rarely find the time to do it...

Still, she was here now, and in her mind
she could see the lovely picture she was
going to paint.

But suddenly the door of her studio flew open and in marched her husband, Prince Wonderful. He was wearing a posh riding outfit.

"So this is where you've been hiding!" he said. "I've been looking for you everywhere, sweetheart. I wondered if you could do me a *teensy* favour?"

"Of course, my love," murmured Snow White, chewing the end of her brush as she thought about how to begin her picture. "What do you want me to do?"

"Oh, nothing much," said Prince Wonderful.
"I need you to pick up my dry cleaning, that's all.
I forgot, and I'm about to go riding with
some friends."

A slight frown crept over Snow White's face. Prince Wonderful could be very forgetful about doing things like that, and part of her just wanted to get on with her picture. But another part thought it wouldn't be nice to say no to her husband. So she put down her brush and smiled.

"No problem, my love," she said. "You run along and have your fun."

"That's great, thanks!" said the prince as he
dashed off.

"See you later!"

Snow White left the palace and headed into town. She felt vaguely miserable, and that made her cross with herself. What right did she have to be unhappy?

Everyone knew her story – the Evil Stepmother hating her…

…the Huntsman letting her live…

...the Seven Dwarves taking her in...

...the Poisoned Apple sending her to sleep...

...the Prince waking her and their magical wedding.

And these days her life was perfect, of course.

Although it would be good to have time to paint as well...

There was a lot of dry cleaning to collect and Snow White wondered how she could carry it all. But as she was leaving she noticed a poster on the shop door.

GRAND PAINTING

COMPETITION

Prizes to be won!

Deadline for entries —

Saturday

Snow White felt very excited, and took down the details. She would love to enter. But then, as she hurried back to the palace, her mind began to fill with doubt. She probably wasn't good enough. Although maybe she should enter anyway. Soon her head was spinning with confusion. What should she *do*?

She badly needed some advice. And suddenly she knew who to ask – the Magic Mirror, the one thing belonging to her stepmother that she had kept.

"Mirror, mirror on the wall," she said. "Should I bother to enter at all?"

"*Go for it girlfriend, don't let this pass by,*"
sang the Magic Mirror, its cloudy surface
shimmering mysteriously. "*Put yourself first and
give it a try.*"

"Er... isn't that the wrong way round?" said
Snow White. "I won't know if I come first
unless I enter. But thanks, you've helped me
make up my mind!"

That night Snow White found it hard to sleep.
She kept thinking about the picture she was going
to create, and how *amazing* she wanted it to be.

She was in her studio bright and early the next morning, getting her paints and brushes ready. She was just about to make a start when her mobile rang.

"Hi there, Snow White!" said a deep voice. "I wondered if you could do me a favour. You know I wouldn't normally ask, but we're really *desperate*."

Snow White's heart sank. She knew instantly the voice belonged to the Huntsman, who was now her friend. He and his wife were lovely people, but they didn't seem to be any good at organising themselves, which meant they often called Snow White for help.

"I'm not sure I can," said Snow White.
"I'm right in the middle of something…"

"Oh, *please*, Snow White," said the Huntsman.
"Mrs Huntsman starts a new job today and
I'm going to the dentist, so we need you to
look after the kids."

Snow White bit her lip. It wouldn't be very nice to say no, would it?

"I'm on my way," she said, putting down her paintbrush with a sigh.

The Huntsman's children were lovely too, but they could also be quite lively, and she ended up babysitting for most of the day. The Huntsman told an exhausted Snow White that he'd bumped into a friend after he'd left the dentist, and they had lost track of the time.

Snow White would have to wait until tomorrow to start her painting. She slept heavily, and it took her a while to get up and into her studio in the morning. But when she stood in front of the blank canvas, her mind began to fill with doubt once more.

She decided it might be a good idea to have
another chat with the Magic Mirror.

"Mirror, mirror, you're so wise," she said.
"Do you think I'll win a prize?"

"*You could be the best, but not this way,*" sang the mirror, its surface less cloudy this time, although still shimmering. "*Just think of yourself today!*"

Snow White frowned – it seemed a strange thing to say – and she went back to staring at her blank canvas. Then suddenly she heard someone knocking at the palace door. She sighed and put down her paintbrush again.

It was Kevin, the youngest of the Seven Dwarves, and he looked worried.

"Hi, Snow White," he said. "The others have sent me to ask for a favour."

"Don't tell me," said Snow White. "You've had one of your arguments?"

Snow White was fond of the Seven Dwarves, and she was grateful to them for taking her in. But the one thing she didn't miss about living with them was the constant arguing.

They fought like cats and dogs, and they were always asking her to come round and sort out their quarrels.

She thought of saying no – but decided that wouldn't be nice. So she went to their house with Kevin and calmed the others down, although it took a while.

The house was in a terrible mess, so she spent the rest of the day tidying up...

...and doing the washing.

She even cooked them a lovely supper before she left.

That night Snow White was very tired, and she felt very fed up too. She slept badly, and got up in the middle of the night to look at her empty canvas again.

The deadline for the competition was only a couple of days away, and she was no closer to getting her picture finished. In fact, she hadn't even *started* it!

"Mirror, mirror, tell me true," she murmured as she sat in the moonlight streaming through her window. "Why is this happening? What shall I do?"

"*I've told you once, I've told you twice,*" the Magic Mirror sang crossly, its surface totally clear this time. "*Face it, girlfriend – you're just TOO nice!*"

Snow White looked into the Magic Mirror, and suddenly understood what it had been trying to make her see. *She would never get any painting done if she kept stopping to help everybody else.*

She realised it might be time to think of herself, although that would mean saying no, and she didn't know if she could...

Snow White soon had a chance to find out. She was in her studio the next day when Prince Wonderful came to ask if she would take his library books back for him.

They were a *year* overdue.

"Er, no, sweetheart, I can't," said Snow White.

"I'm actually rather busy."

"Oh, right you are," said the prince, looking surprised. "Well, not to worry."

Snow White said no a lot over the next
two days…

...and she got her painting done in time for the competition.

She was *very* happy when she won!

And strangely enough, once she began to say no, the people in her life began doing more for themselves too.

Snow White was still nice, but now she had time to do things she enjoyed.

And so she lived…

HAPPILY EVER AFTER!